Santa and the Goodnight Train

June Sobel

Illustrated by Laura Huliska-Beith

Houghton Mifflin Harcourt

Boston   New York

hmhbooks.com

The illustrations in this book were done in acrylic paints with fabric and paper collage.
The display lettering was created by Laura Huliska-Beith.
The text type was set in Pink Martini.

Library of Congress Cataloging-in-Publication Data is on file.
Names: Sobel, June, author. | Huliska-Beith, Laura, 1964- illustrator.
Title: Santa and the Goodnight Train / June Sobel : illustrated by Laura
Huliska-Beith.
Description: Boston : New York : Houghton Mifflin Harcourt, [2019] | Series:
Goodnight Train | Summary: Illustrations and easy-to-read, rhyming text
welcome riders onto the Goodnight Train as it follows Santa's sleigh on
Christmas Eve.
Identifiers: LCCN 2018052152 | ISBN 9781328618405 (hardcover picture book)
Subjects: | CYAC: Stories in rhyme. | Railroad trains--Fiction. |
Christmas--Fiction. | Santa Claus--Fiction. | Bedtime--Fiction.
Classification: LCC PZ8.3.S692 San 2019 | DDC [E]--dc23
LC record available at https://lccn.loc.gov/2018052152
ISBN: 978-1-328-61840-5

Manufactured in China
SCP 10 9 8 7 6 5 4 3
4500826667

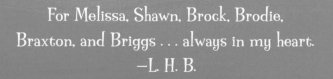

To my Bestlake Tribe
who all enjoy a visit from Santa!
—J. S.

For Melissa, Shawn, Brock, Brodie,
Braxton, and Briggs . . . always in my heart.
—L. H. B.

Santa's coming! Ho! Ho! Ho!
The Goodnight Train is all aglow!

Engine's shined, looking jolly.
Strung with lights, decked with holly.

The porter checks the tickets twice.
Who's been naughty? Who's been nice?

All aboard! Slow and steady.
Careful not to drop your teddy!

Jammies on! It's Christmas Eve!
Snug in bed. We're set to leave.

On the track, train cars sway,
keeping watch for Santa's sleigh.

Up above, we spy a hoof.
Is that Santa on the roof?

Ring-a-ling! Ring-a-ling!
Whoooo! Whoooo!

Race through a town of gingerbread!
Gumdrop Crossing straight ahead!

Candy canes line the street.
Every house a tasty treat!

There's a bite out of a star!
Can Santa Claus be very far?

Fa La La! Fa La La!
Chooo! Chooo!

Dashing through the woods at night,
the merry train shines a light.

Chipmunks dance. Squirrels cheer.
"Santa Claus has just been here!"

But where, oh where did Santa go?
Who made that angel in the snow?

HO! HO! HO! HO! HO! HO!
Whoooo! Whoooo!

The engineer hits the brake!
Everyone is wide awake!

Santa's sleigh is on the tracks.
Reindeer yawning on their backs!

Santa Claus is counting sheep!
One reindeer is fast asleep!

"Wake up! Wake up! Move the sled!
All aboard! Come find your bed!"

Jingle! Jingle! Jingle! Jingle!
To·o·o·o·ot! To·o·o·o·ot!

Faster! Faster! The train wheels roll.
Conductor yells, "Next stop: North Pole!"

At the workshop, elves all cheer.
Santa's here until next year!

Before he goes, there's one last toy
in his bag for a sleepy boy.

The Goodnight Train chugs off to leave,
heading home on Christmas Eve.

Fa La La! Fa La La!
Sleeeeeep!

NORTH POLE

Good night, Santa!

Good night, train!